I0566041

A LIFE,
IN LETTERS

A story of resilience, sequins, and hope

Rodney Rhoda Taylor

CRESTINGWAVE
PUBLISHING

A LIFE, IN LETTERS

by Rodney Rhoda Taylor

Copyright © 2024 Rodney Rhoda Taylor

For information about the author or to receive copies of the book for review, please send an email to:
pub@gocwpub.com

Book Design by Rodney Taylor and Lazar Kackarovski
Edited by Kris Neely
Cover Design: Brian R. Barilleaux

Printed in the United States of America
First Printing, 2024

ISBN: 978-1-956048-24-7

Published by Cresting Wave Publishing, LLC.

"We publish the books you <u>need</u> to read."

Other works by Rodney Rhoda Taylor

P.S. I Love You, a short play in *SF Here I Come! Anthology*

Motherly Advice, a short play in *#WTFamily Anthology*

WITH APPRECIATION

This book began life as a college assignment many years ago and only saw the light of day because I was working on another book and got sidetracked with this one. Honestly, I didn't know where to go with this or if I would finish it.

Thank you, Rich, for encouraging me to continue exploring what this could become and for suggesting the last-minute name change. Who knows what would have happened if you hadn't said it sounded like a good idea?

Thank you, Allison, for being my sounding board and reading this throughout development.

And thank you, Andrea, for being my third set of eyes and catching everything I didn't.

And Maggie, I'm sorry for making you cry. But am I?

RRT

CONTENTS

With Appreciation 4

Contents. 5

Authors Note 7

Dedication 8

THE INNOCENT YEARS 9

THE AWKWARD YEARS 17

THE DETERMINED & OPTIMISTIC YEARS 43

REALITY SETS IN YEARS 67

THE QUEST FOR PEACE YEARS 89

MY TRUE SELF YEARS 117

About the Author 139

AUTHORS NOTE

A *Life, In Letters,* is a memoir of sorts. It is a collection of letters written about the thoughts, feelings, and emotions that have influenced my life.

It's also an emotional journey through puberty, coming out, and how one line from the *Torch Song Trilogy* shaped how I dealt with those who didn't like or agree with whom I love.

It tells of my quest for love, my battle with depression, and my complex relationship with masculinity—whatever that is. It's about being inspired by Billy Porter, conquering my fear of rejection and loss, and learning to find inner peace.

But most importantly, it's a story of hope because even on the darkest days, there is always a shiny disco ball at the end of the tunnel. And a fabulous pair of pumps. And a sparkling caftan, waiting to be worn and to be seen.

On reflection, who would you write to if you were to write a letter or letters to the thoughts, feelings, and emotions or an event that helped shape your life?

What would you say?

DEDICATION

**To my aunt,
Joan Smalling.**

THE
INNOCENT
YEARS

deer Santa,

how are you? how are rain deer? how is Rudoff? i hope you and elfs okay.

Mummy say i write you so you know what i want for Christmas. i hope okay. i want a babee go by by, raggy andy, a big wheel, and a tedy bear.

merry christmas,

luv you

Dear Santa,

I hope you remember me? i write you last year.

Thank you for the toys you bring me. i very muchd like them.

How are you and elfs? how are rain deer? i hope you all doing great.

I been a good boy. i do everyfing mummy and daddy tell me. i eat my vegables. i don't like vegables thay are yucky. my father took my baby go by by away from me. he said boys don't play with dolls. but I like playing with dolls. my brother is also mean to me i hope he's on the notty list. i nice to him.

For Christmas id like tiny people thay are little toy people and thay have an airplan and house and farm. can i get those? i want some weebels wabels. thay don't fall down. that's what comersal say weebels wabels but thay don't fall down. it is a funny saying. i also like Evil kanevil, racing cars and racing tracks, and some cars?

Merry xtmas,

Your friend

P.s. mommy say i leave you snacks. what you like? i love cookies and milk, so i'll leave you cookies and milk.

Dear Santa,

I hope you had a great year. I hope you, the elves, and the raindeer are okay. How is Mrs. Clause? I hope she's okay. Did you enjoy the cookies I left you last year? Thank you for the presents. I got some I didn't ask for, and that was nice.

I been good again this year, not like my brother. He still mean. He shuld be on notty list. I started school this year, I don't like. They give me things I have to do, and I can't play with my toys. That not nice. I was sick this year in the hospital. That was no fun.

For Christmas, can I have the six million dollar man toy? He's a boy doll, so my daddy should like that. I like how he has powers and can run really fast and see things with his eye. Can I also have Barbie and her camper and a Play dough set?

Merry Christmas. Your friend.

P.s. Sorry I forgot treats for the raindeer. I leave carots for them this year I hope they like carots.

Dear Santa,

How are you? How is Mrs. Clause? How are raindeer? I hope Rudoff is ok.

I have been a good boy again. I get good grades in school. I like it a little more this year.

Mommy said I don't tell you my brother is mean. She says that is tatell telling and you don't like that. I hope I am not on the notty list. I'm really a good boy. I'm still doing what my parents tell me, and I eat all my vegetables. They are still yucky.

I like a train set, Lincoln logs, and tinker toys for Christmas this year. Can I also have the Snoopy teddy bear? I like teddy bears.

Merry Christmas to you and Mrs. Clause and all the elves.

PS I'd also like a Cher doll. She is pretty and I love her dresses. Can you leave her in my room instead of by tree? That's so I won't get in trouble asking for a doll.

Dear Santa,

My brother says you don't exist, but I don't believe him because you keep bringing me presents I want for Christmas. So, you have to exist, don't you? He says Mom and Dad bring me presents, but the only things I get from them are clothes. You don't bring me clothes, so they can't be you.

Are the elves doing okay this year? How is Rudolf? Should I leave something for the elves again?

For Christmas this year, can you bring R2D2, a Dr. Kit, a big Godzilla toy, and a bicycle with colorful stringers on the handlebars? Oh, and a BB gun because that's what boys are supposed to want. Merry Christmas, Santa

Your Friend

Dear How Boys Should Act,

I'm writing to you this year instead of Santa because my brother said he doesn't exist, and well, I don't think he can help me with my problem anyway. See, I'm a little confused, and I'm hoping you can help me. People keep telling me I shouldn't act the way I do. They say I act like a girl, but I don't know what that means. The kids at school and my brother call me names and push and shove me because of the way I act. My brother also hits me, which hurts when he does. I got a bruise once because of him. I told Mom, but she said I must have done something to deserve to be hit. But I didn't.

My Dad is also mean to me. Once, he started to hit me because he said I was acting like a girl. He said he would beat it out of me if I didn't stop it. It really hurt. Mom finally yelled at him to stop. He's always yelling at me and telling me to stop acting the way I do, but I don't understand what is wrong with the way I am.

Maybe can you please tell me how I should be acting? I want people to stop calling me names. I'd also like it if I didn't get beat up as much. If you'd help me, I'd be happy if you could.

Thank You. Signed,

I Don't Understand

P, S, How long do bruises last?

THE
AWKWARD
YEARS

Dear How Boys Should Act,

The name calling has gotten worse now that I'm in junior high.

Every day, kids at school are calling me names like faggot, queer, or freak. They keep saying I'm gay. But I'm not! At least, I don't think I am.

I didn't even know what that meant until I looked it up in the dictionary. It's when a boy likes another boy. But I don't like other boys! At least, I don't think I do. Well, I'm not sure. I guess I think other boys are cute, but what's wrong with that?

I only know that I wish I didn't have to go to school anymore. Getting picked on and made fun of every day hurts. My brother is still hitting me and calling me names as well. He always makes fun of me because I'm different and don't act like you.

I wish I was like the other boys. They like hunting, fishing, and playing sports, but I don't like to do any of those things. I can't kill Bambi; fish are just slimy and gross, and sports, I don't understand what all the hype is about. Guys running around chasing each other to tackle them to the ground does not sound fun. I want to point out that they are the ones chasing other guys, not me, and yet they call me the gay one! I'm trying to avoid contact with other boys as much as possible because I don't want the other kids saying bad things about me more than they already do.

And I really hate gym class.

Anyways, what am I supposed to do? I hope you can help because I don't like them calling me what they do. I'd like to be like everyone else. Am I gay?

Thank you,

Confused

Dear Puberty,

What the hell! I've got hair growing in places I shouldn't, my voice is cracking when I talk, making me sound funnier than I normally do, and a certain body part keeps getting hard all of the time!

I walk into a classroom, not even thinking of anything, and the next thing I know, super erecto! Or I'm in Spanish class listening to the teacher talk about verb conjugation, and out of nowhere, boom, another one. Again! *WHY?!*

The damn thing has a mind of its own. It's embarrassing. I hope no one notices.

Thank God I don't have gym class anymore. Otherwise, I'd be screwed when it came time to shower! This is all your fault, by the way. If it weren't for you, I wouldn't have to worry about hair growing in strange places or when the next random pop-up will happen. Luckily, we have a sex ed class in school soon. Hopefully, they can tell me why this stuff is happening, especially since you haven't bothered to say a word about it.

Just so you know, I like to be prepared for things! And I can't be ready if I don't know what's going to happen! So, if you have any other revelations in store for me, please share them!

I don't think I can handle any more surprises . . .

Thanks,

Really Freaked Out

PS So that you know, the next random pop-up just happened. Stop it already!

Dear Puberty,

What the hell! You clearly didn't read my last letter, and if you did, you didn't pay ANY attention to it because I specifically said I don't like *surprises*! But that's all that seems to be happening these days.

First it was the hair appearing in places it had never been before. I wasn't prepared for that, but okay. Then there was the voice cracking, which went higher instead of going deeper like the other boys! OK! I'm trying to deal with that. Then there were the random pop-ups. I'm STILL waiting for a reason why they keep happening.

Now, if all of that wasn't bad enough, you go and throw one more thing at me: WHAT THE HELL WAS UP WITH THAT DREAM?!!

I don't *know how to describe what happened, but whatever it was, it ruined everything*—and I mean **everything**! I need new PJs now because of it.

You gotta tell me: is that what happens when one dreams about kissing another boy? All I can remember about the dream was that I was kissing another guy. Not sure who it was. But he was hot. Then things started to get, well, a little bit more intimate, if you will, between the two of us. We were rubbing our crotches against each other. I started rubbing my hands over his chest, and then I slowly started to move my hands down his stomach to his pants.

As I started to undo them and right before I was able to see what his dick looked like, BOOM, the weirdest sensation came over me. The next thing I knew, the front of my PJs was covered in something. I don't know what, but they were covered in something! I didn't know what happened. I jumped out of bed and ran to the shower. I'm really freaked out now!

Why didn't you tell me this was going to happen? Is it going to happen again? You have got to stop keeping things like this from me. Does it happen to other boys? If so, I guess I'm finally like them now. It took long enough, but somehow, I don't think they're dreaming about kissing other boys.

If I'm dreaming about boys, does that mean what I think it means? That what the kids are saying about me is true? That I'm gay? If the dream tells anything, then I guess I really do like boys.

Is it going to happen again? The dream, and what happened during it? Any words of wisdom on what to do about any of this would be helpful.

Thanks,

Still Freaking Out

P.S. I think I figured out who the guy was.

Dear Puberty,

We finally had that sex ed class! Now I know what the hell is going on with my body. Turns out I'm not the only one going through a "change."

Ugh, none of this sounds fun. It sounds like it's going to be a rather painful experience. Is there any way I can skip it? I know, silly question, considering I'm already in the middle of this god-awful experience. Gee—I can't wait for acne! Which, as you know, is one of the great side effects of all these raging hormones. Of course, thank you for that, by the way. Add it to the list of things the other kids can make fun of me for.

At least I now know why I had that dream. It was a huge relief to know that it happens to all boys. By the way, a warning would have been really appreciated. Well, I guess I did have a warning.

Does that feeling happen every time before it, well, you know, before that happens? They didn't tell us in class, and I wasn't even gonna ask. I didn't want anyone to know that that happened.

They also discussed the whole boys liking other boys thing. It's a relief to know I'm not the only one with these feelings. But they also said that boys liking other boys wasn't natural because boys weren't supposed to like other boys. Now I finally understand why everyone has been giving me such a tough time for years now.

But! Why am I dreaming about other boys if feeling this way isn't natural? And why did my body react the way it did in the dream? This is so confusing. My body is telling me one thing, what and who it likes, while other people are telling me that what I'm feeling is wrong. If my body is telling me that I find boys attractive, then shouldn't I be doing what my body likes and what feels natural to me?

Ugh, all I know is that I shouldn't say anything to anyone else about this because of how they might react.

Does this get any better?

Thanks,

Confused

P.S. Are these random pop-ups ever going to stop?

Dear Fairy Godmother,

I'm writing to you today because, well, I have to get something off my chest, and since I have no one else to talk to about this, I figured you'd be the best person to speak to. I live in a small town, and for years now, the kids at school have said I'm gay because of the way I act. I didn't know what that meant at the time other than they were just being mean and making fun of me.

It's only recently that I found out that being gay is when a guy likes another guy, and in this town, that is most definitely frowned upon. They say it's not natural, but why do I have these feelings if it's not natural? It feels natural to me to like other guys, and this has been my dilemma for a while now. People are telling me one thing, that what I feel is wrong, but my body and how I feel inside are telling me something completely different. This, as you can imagine, has just been damn confusing. But the time has finally come when I need to be honest with myself, especially about this whole liking other boys issue.

For as long as I can remember, I've always thought other guys were attractive. Still, because of how people treated me, I've been too afraid to acknowledge or even think about how I feel toward other guys. Then puberty arrived, and well, my body revealed *all kinds* of things about myself. The main one is that I definitely like the male physique better than I ever will like the female body.

So, after a lot of reflection, here we are. I'm about to acknowledge something I've always been too afraid to do: I do like other guys. *Oh, that was weird.*

Finally, admitting something after so long is like lifting a weight off my shoulders. But at the same time, it hasn't been lifted because I still can't be myself. I still have to hide how I feel because of other people.

Ugh. Well, at least I know who I am, and that's all that matters, right? I have to be me, and that's the important thing—at least to me. I hope this gets easier.

Sincerely,

No Longer Confused

Dear Crush,

I'm not sure how to say this other than to come right out and say it. I think you're cute.

I've kept that a secret far too long—and it started driving me crazy. I sit behind you in U.S. History, which is my favorite subject. But you don't seem too excited to be there as you keep asking to copy my homework. Of course, I let you. I mean, who wouldn't let the football team captain copy their homework, right?!

The few times we've talked have always been the highlight of my day. Just to have those few moments of looking into your beautiful blue eyes has always been a thrill.

In those brief seconds, no one else exists, just the two of us. You ask me out for a date, I say yes, and then we go out, and you are my first kiss. Then the school bell rings, and the brief moment of the world just being the two of us fades away, and reality kicks in. Crap!

We're both guys, and you would probably freak out if you knew I liked you that way. I wish I could tell you how I feel, but I can't because you might beat me up, and I'd like to avoid that at all costs. Getting beat up, that is. But I'd love to go out with you if you feel the same way.

Ugh, I wish this were easier. I wish you didn't sit in front of me in class. I wish for all kinds of things, but the one thing I really wish for is that you'd ask me out, but I know that will never happen.

Thinking of you,

Admirer

PS I love how your Wranglers fit you so nicely. You have a great butt. By the way, can I have my homework assignment back? I don't want to fail the class.

Dear Fairy Godmother,

Well, I've finally graduated from high school, and can I say what a relief it is to know that I will never have to see those people again. Oh my god, that was an absolute nightmare. Being called faggot and queer every day by everyone hasn't endeared any of them to me. And none of those people are on my list of people I want to stay connected with.

Well, there is one person, but I don't think that will happen. I'm not sure I'm his ... type.

Does being gay get any easier now? Will I finally get to meet other gay people?

So, where do gay people live? I know it is not in this area. Other kids said San Francisco is a big gay city. Is that true? If so, I should move there. Someday. But for now, I'm stuck here in this hell hole.

At least I have something new to try: I'm starting college in the fall. My big hope is that people are a lot nicer there. And I hope I finally get to meet others like me.

It'd be nice not to be the only gay person in this area.

Thanks for listening,

Lonely

Dear Crush,

I thought I'd never see you again once we graduated from high school, but then you walked into my Algebra class. I can't tell you how surprised and happy that made me. I didn't think you would notice me, but then your beautiful blue eyes saw me, and the smile that lit up your face showed you recognized me.

When you sat next to me and said "Hi," I swear my heart about stopped beating right then and there. The entire world disappeared, and it was just the two of us.

Since then, I've looked forward to attending class, and I don't really like algebra! It isn't easy to understand. How do people use it anyway?

I was happy to see you and talk to you almost daily. I wanted to tell you how I felt, but deep down inside, I knew I couldn't, as I didn't want to, I don't know, maybe, frighten you off. That evening, you came over to my dorm room and studied with me — wow, that was the best night of my life. I couldn't believe you wanted to study with me. Me of all people, the one everyone made fun of in high school. You wanted to study with me. It was like my dream had finally come true, which it had. Well, sort of.

I wish I had been braver that night. You moved one time, changing how you were sitting, and I swear I thought I saw your hard dick pressing against your jeans. I just glanced. I don't think you saw me looking. What would you have done if I said something about it? Would you have been okay with that?

I don't know. Maybe I should have.

You've become distant since then. Did I say something wrong? Did you want to do something as well? I wish this were easier. And that I could tell you how I feel.

Thinking of you,

Your Crushee

Dear Fairy Godmother,

Oh My God, it finally happened!

I met another gay person.

He's just like me, noticeably effeminate. He works in one of those novelty kitchen stores in the mall. One day, I was walking by his store when I saw him. I can't tell you how excited I was to spot another gay person finally! I didn't think there were others like me in this area, but sure enough, there are! I wanted to go in, say hi, and introduce myself, but I was too afraid to do so, so I left.

I went back a few days later, and this time, I went in—but before I could say anything, *he approached me and introduced himself.* We instantly hit it off; it was like we'd known each other our entire life and become best friends. He's telling me all about what it's like to be gay and how to deal with people who don't like us. I'm also learning about all the crucial gay lingo, like what a queen is, what tops and bottoms are, what poppers are, and what it's really like to have sex. We are not having sex. He's just telling me all about it.

More importantly, he told me about Cher's significance, which explains why I wanted her doll as a kid. He's also filled me in on all the other divas: Barbra Streisand, Bette Midler, Judy Garland, and Madonna! I'm learning so much. It's nice to know that I'm no longer the only one in the world. Thank you for answering my wish!

With love,

No Longer Lonely

p.s. I never did get my Cher doll as a kid.

Dear Closet,

It's time I leave your protective services and head into the world as an out and proud Gay man. But you already knew that! The gay part, not the heading out into the world part, as I just told you that.

Hell. Who am I kidding—we both know I've never been "hiding." It's kind of hard to hide the fact that I'm not the "manliest" of men, hence the reason everyone has assumed I'm gay to begin with. Since everyone has always "assumed," do I really need to come out? What's the point?

I've been thinking about this whole "coming out" thing. I think it's stupid. Why can't I love who I want without being judged? I already know what you'll say because people aren't that accepting. I know. *I know!* If I can be honest, I'm afraid to do it. Telling people, not the being gay part. I can't wait to do…that!

But what happens if they reject me and stop loving me because I'm different? Again, I know what you're going to say: loving someone of the same sex doesn't make me different. Having three arms or two heads makes me different, which I don't have, so I'm not different. (See, I <u>do</u> listen to you.)

You made this whole coming out thing sound…easy. It's not. It's scary. Telling people and not knowing how they are going to react makes it feel like I'm jumping off a damn cliff. Hell, at least if I jump off a cliff, I can see the ground coming up to meet me until I go *splat*. In this situation, I'll just be jumping into the abyss...

And hoping for the best: acceptance.

Ugh! I know—take a deep breath and relax. "I'm Gay."

There.

I said it.

As I say those words, I hear your voice a thousand times telling me it's okay to love who I want.

I'm Gay. There, I said it again.

I'M GAY!

As I write those words, it does feel good to say them.

Out.

Loud.

Wow. I feel a little freer as if I'm no longer confined. Oh my God! That's why they call it coming out of the closet—I'm no longer imprisoned. I'm not saying you imprisoned me. It's more like I've been detained, held hostage, imprisoned by society and what they say I should be, and I will never be what society, or my family, thinks I *should* be.

And I have you to thank for that.

You've helped me realize that this is <u>my</u> life and that the only person I need to make happy is me! I'm Gay. That's so freeing.

So, now. What...?

I tell the family.

They have a meltdown.

I go on and live my life.

And ... then what?

Are gay guys going to throw themselves at me, begging for dates? I heard there's an annual Gay parade. Is this where people who have come out are celebrated? Or are they celebrating?

All right!

I know I'm procrastinating. It's what I do, especially with this topic... are you super 100% sure this is the right thing to do? *Hell.*

Thank you.

Grateful, but Hesitant

Dear Virginia Ham,

While I know I'm just a stranger to you, please know that I write this letter with appreciation and gratitude. You have helped me to come out. Finally.

OK, let me explain why.

A while back, I finally admitted to myself that I'm gay. I hate saying that… "I've admitted it to myself." Like I've struggled with it. Truth be told, I've never *struggled* with being gay. I've been this way for as long as I can remember, and I've always been okay with it, as this is how I am.

No, the struggle for me has been my fear of others rejecting me when I tell them, and this is where you come into the picture. I saw your movie, *Torch Song Trilogy*, the other day, and I cannot tell you how much of an effect it had on me. After watching your film, I'm no longer hesitant to come out or of people's reactions when I do because of what you told your mother in one scene.

You said she wouldn't have a place in your life if she could not give you the love and respect you deserve. That one little sentence—has completely changed my perspective on coming out. I had always thought I had to do and be whatever I could to be in people's lives. It never occurred to me until that moment that it was the opposite.

That scene reminded me I have power and control over who stays or goes from my life.

While that may be one sentence, it carries a lot of truth and power for me. I have now adopted it as my motto for life, "Like me and love me for who I am."

And if not, then you do not get to be in my life. Thank you for that. And thank you for creating a movie that shows that gay people are as ordinary as everyone else. You have helped a little gay boy to come out of the closet finally.

With much love and appreciation,

Inspired

Dear Ex-Best Friend,

I was, well, surprised by your reaction when I told you I'm gay, especially since I flew all the way to England to see you.

I guess I should have listened to you on the phone when you said you did not want to talk about it. I thought we had a bond that would last forever due to our friendship and what we had been through in high school, with both of us being the oddballs – at least according to the rest of the school.

The joke was on me because you threw our friendship out the window like it meant … nothing to you.

I was a bit taken aback when you told me you did not want to hear anything about my life and that the only thing we could talk about was you and what you wanted. At that moment, I realized you were not the person I knew from two years before. The military changed you, or it was your prejudicial religious background finally coming through.

But being that selfish and dictating what we could talk about to make you feel more comfortable is not a friendship I can be a part of. Friendships are not supposed to be one-sided; they are supposed to be loving and supportive *on both sides*. Believe me when I say ending our friendship hurts more than you know, but I can't be friends with someone as narrow-minded and selfish as you are.

I will say this, however: there was no better place to end a friendship than a quaint English village.

By the time you get this letter, I will have left this wonderful little village and will be in London for the next week. If you desire to be friends, that is where you will find me. If I do not hear from you, then I wish you a good life.

Truly,

Your *Gay* Friend

Dear Darkness? . . .

Please forgive me if I've gotten your name wrong. We've never been properly introduced, so I don't know what to call you.

I'm writing to you because I've felt you hanging around lately, and your appearances are very memorable as you tend to (and please don't take this the wrong way), but you tend to suck all of the energy and happiness out of a room as well as myself.

Of course, this leaves me feeling washed out. It's like a dark cloud has descended upon me, taking away my desire to do anything. When you finally go, I'm left with a feeling of complete emptiness and nothingness.

And it takes me a while to recover and feel like myself again. I've never felt that way before, and I hope I don't feel that way again.

So, I don't mean to be rude, but PLEASE STOP coming around. I'm just now putting myself together from that visit. And I'd rather not experience that again. Once was enough.

Take care,

Not Your Friend

THE DETERMINED

& OPTIMISTIC

YEARS

Dear Adulthood,

I did it!

I finally completed my pre-adult work and am now ready for whatever you've got in store for me. But hang on for a minute—for the record, that pre-work *was not* the easiest stuff to get through. Especially high school. That was a rather horrible experience, but I figure if I can make it through the name-calling, the pushing, the shoving, and the bitchy judgment from the mean girls who dictated how one's high school life was going to be, then I can make it through whatever you've got in store for me.

So, what do you got? I know that's "bad grammar," but that really just shows the extent of my education. I hope it's okay if I ask that question, especially since we've never met, but I figure it can't hurt to ask. OK, well, shit. To be honest, I'm asking because ... I'm one of those people who has to have everything planned out. I'm not particularly good at "going with the flow."

I'm sure this is the result of some long-ago, long-hidden childhood trauma that will be unpacked in some stupid therapy session at some point. Of which, is that part of this whole adulting thing, dealing with childhood stuff my parents inflected on me? If so, can I make a request for a job that pays good money so I can pay for the countless hours of that therapy I'm probably going to need?

And besides counseling, what else can I expect? Other bills for a lifestyle I can't afford? Love? Heartbreak? Joy? Sadness? Nights of drinking with friends and a hangover that lasts throughout the next day? Or is a life filled with bad decisions, lots of regret, and a co-dependent nature in the cards for me? I know it's a lot of questions, but I'm simply curious as to what the grand plan is going to be.

There is a plan, right? I mean, damn, *there has to be a plan!* I hope you aren't going to just get this whole life thing started and then make up a plan as you go along! No. Please see above where I said I'm not exceptionally good at that stuff. No, you can't just expect me to wing it! I don't function well in those types of situations. I need to have everything planned so I know how to deal with things. Surprises and me, we don't get along too well at all. That's the reason why *everything* in my life needs to be planned! Planning helps decrease my anxiety. I know, deep breath.

Anyway, thank you for your time and attention to my letter. I look forward to hearing back from you and starting this whole journey.

Sincerely,

Young and Hopeful

p.s. Is next week too early to expect your response?

Dear Closet,

I did it. I told the family that I am gay.

Yeah. It went the way I thought it would: Mom said she suspected ...well, *duh*. Dad was disappointed and disowned me (no surprise there either!) My brother, well, he doesn't want me to be around him or his kids because he's afraid they'll grow up and be gay, just like their uncle. Like that's going to happen. It's not like some germ you can catch.

One doesn't BECOME this fabulous; one is BORN this way! And yes, that's my way of covering up that it hurts like a bitch. But as we've said in the past, I don't have room for that shit in my life. I can't, and I won't do it. *Got* to adhere to my motto: love and accept me, or you aren't part of my life. Yes, that sounds harsh, but as you and I both know, it's about survival. The rest of the family was just waiting for me to confirm their suspicions.

Like I said earlier, one can't be this fabulous and hide it from others. As far as everyone else, like friends from high school, I didn't stay in touch with anyone, but I'm sure they'll find out in due time. Maybe my crush will finally admit (if only to himself!) that he feels the same way. I know, wishful thinking.

Anyway, after coming out, I moved to the big city of Portland. Okay, compared to San Francisco, it's not that big. But it's a good first move away from my home place. And can I just say, *Holy Crap!* It is an entirely different world out there. There are drag bars, leather bars, dive bars, lesbian bars, and "brunch"—where everyone drinks Mimosas! Unfortunately, I can't partake in this rite of passage because I'm allergic to champagne, but I can do a Bloody Mary!

Since coming out, life has been an eye-opening experience. And I have enjoyed ... every *minute* of it. The highlight so far has been attending my very first Gay Pride parade. *WOW!* That is all I can say about that. Well! Walking down the street with hundreds of other gay people and seeing other people lined up on the sidewalks *in support of us* was an experience that I will never forget. Coming from a small town like I did, I only experienced how much people hate us. But seeing everyone out in support brought tears to my eyes. I never imagined so many people actually loved and supported us. It was a day that will forever be in my heart.

Yes—life has definitely opened up and become a *completely* different experience for me since I came out. And I have you to thank 100% for that. You always encouraged me and told me nothing was wrong with loving another man. Thank you for that and for always being there for me.

With Love,

Out and Proud

Dear Cupid,

What do I need to do to get this whole romance thing started? Are there forms I need to fill out? Do I send you a headshot? Questions I need to answer? Are there fees I need to pay?

Sorry, I didn't mean to jump right in and ask you all kinds of questions. I'm just eager to begin dating. So, if it's okay with you, I'll just go ahead and tell you about the guy I'm looking for, and that way, you won't be going into this search blindfolded. So here goes.

I'm looking for someone friendly, caring, sensitive, and with a great sense of humor. I mean, I'm funny, and he needs to laugh at my jokes. He should also be romantic—you know, candlelit dinners, long walks on the beach, holding hands, and sharing our dreams. He should also like to cuddle. That's especially important to me.

Physically, I'd like a guy a little taller than me so he can wrap his arms around me and hold me tight as we kiss. It'd be nice if he had a toned physique, as who doesn't like a guy with muscles? But not too big of muscles as all the other men would be throwing themselves at him, and I don't want to have to beat the bitches back. But I will if I have to!

Oh, and one of the most crucial things he has to have is a hairy chest! This is necessary, as it's a huge turn-on. Don't get me wrong, smooth and toned is nice, especially if he has a six-pack, but he'll have to go when we're done doing the deed. I just don't see any longevity with a smooth guy. The hairier, the better. Oh, and if he's bald, we've struck gold, as my ideal man is bald with a hairy chest. Oh my God, that would be perfect! Or should I say dreamy?

I'm not too particular about his profession as long as we both make enough money to own a house, have two dogs, and travel. Now, with that said, if you happen to find me a nice Jewish doctor or a lawyer, I'd be okay with that. What mom wouldn't like to say her son-in-law is a doctor or a lawyer? (OK, mine wouldn't, but this is about me and not her.)

So, there you have it, my ideal guy. Now, what happens? Do I continue to go about my daily activities, and he'll just appear? Do I need to go someplace special so he can "bump" into me? What do I need to do next? Please let me know if you need anything else from me to help with your search.

Thank you so much for your attention and (hopefully eager) participation,

Looking for Love

p.s. I almost forgot! Now, regarding his … equipment. I hope I'm not being too specific when I say this, but he needs to be big enough, you know, but not too big—because if he is, not too much can happen because too big is just too … much. Thanks for understanding!

My Dearest Drag Divas,

I had the pleasure of seeing your show the other night, and I must say, I was mesmerized! The glitz, the glamour, the sequins, the jewels, and the hair. The. Very. BIG. Hair! It was incredible. And the way you worked the crowd? Amazing! You had everyone eating out of the palms of your bejeweled hands.

How do you guys...sorry, how do you *ladies* do that? You were stunning, and I'm in awe of what you do. That said, I need to come clean and be honest with you. I ... had never seen a drag show until that night, and from the moment the house lights went down, and the pre-show music started, I waited in ready anticipation for the curtains to open and reveal your beauty.

And when they did—there you were! Standing center stage, bathed in the spotlight, shining, and twinkling like the stars in the heavens. I was captivated! Mesmerized! And when the music started and you began performing, I was instantly lost in the show's magic. You were the sheer essence of the glamorous days of Hollywood when the leading ladies were ladies and carried themselves with poise, grace, and elegance.

Seeing you that night awoke an inner diva I did not know existed. Well, that's not exactly true. I knew I had an inner diva; it's just that I've been ashamed of her. I thought if people knew I wanted to wear shiny dresses and sparkling jewelry, they would make fun of me even more than they do now. So, I tried to … ignore her.

Plus, I thought I was the only one who wanted to wear dresses and heels. I didn't realize others felt like I did until I saw your show that night. I mean, you were right there, doing what I was always told was "unacceptable." You were embracing your glamorous side, and not only that, you were showing it to the world … in a spotlight! You showed me that embracing that side of myself is okay! And, honestly, I must say I love wearing heels. They make my legs look *sooooo* good!

Thank you for showing me that my inner diva is not to be feared or ashamed of. She should be embraced, and I should let her out for the entire world to see because someone that marvelous cannot stay hidden from the world!

Your show was indeed an inspiration! I only hope that, in time, I will be as fabulous as all of you. I would appreciate any words of inspiration or pointers you have for me to become as great as you are.

May you be blessed with the powers of Judy, Barbra, Bette, Cher, and Madonna!

Thank you for your time,

Young Drag Queen

p.s. Is there a limit on how high the hair should be?

Dear Friend with Benefits,

I still remember that night like it was yesterday. You were leaving the party, and I, in a rare moment of confidence, approached you and asked if you'd like to get together sexually. We'd been friends for a while, and I figured I might as well give it a shot. I'd been attracted to you for some time...a handsome, bald, hairy-chested man has that effect on me. And what was your response?

You had to think about it. Ouch.

My pride was hurt, as I was hoping you felt the same way about me as I felt about you. Then, to my surprise, you called a few days later with your answer: YES! My heart nearly jumped out of my chest when I got your message. You did feel the same way about me! Well, sort of. You at least wanted to have sex with me, so I was happy with that. I called you back within seconds. I didn't want you to change your mind. We discussed the ground rules: sex only because we didn't want to mess up our friendship, and then a date was set. The weeks passed, and then the night finally arrived. I showered and spent an hour trying to pick out the perfect outfit! Tight jeans to accentuate my cute butt and a shirt that would bring out my green eyes.

You greeted me at the door with a brief kiss, we relaxed over cocktails, and then you grabbed my hand and led me into your bedroom. The rest of the evening was a blur of sexual energy at a level that I was not expecting. We were in tune with each other's bodies and instinctively knew how to bring each other a smile and a sigh. We then lay there—after hours of exploring each other's bodies. The sound of our heavy breathing filled the room. I had dreamed of that moment for months, just lying there, being wrapped in your arms, running my fingers through your hairy chest. I was in heaven.

Our private rendezvous continued over the next several months. We talked, we cuddled, our friendship grew, the sex became more meaningful, and my feelings went from like to ... falling for you. But I kept my feelings to myself out of fear of losing you as a friend.

Then, one night, in an alcohol-infused call, you confessed you had fallen in love with me. Not knowing what to do, I tried to guide our conversation to neutral ground because you were drunk. But in truth, I was in love with you as well. I didn't want to tell you as I wasn't sure how you would react in the state you were in.

I should have told you and invited you over to talk in person. But I didn't, and I regret doing so, as I haven't heard from you since that night. I hope you haven't closed your heart to what could be between us.

I don't want to lose you as a friend or lover. Can we try again?

Missed Opportunity

Death-You Cruel Bastard,

You visited my friend last night, and now you can just FUCK RIGHT OFF!

I can't believe you took *him* from us!

His mother and sisters are devastated, as am I and *everyone* who loved him.

Stay away from me and *never* come anywhere near my life again!

Shattered

Dear Masculinity,

I'm writing to you hoping you can tell me more about yourself. For years, I've been told I don't act enough like you, but when I ask people who you are, no one can give me a definitive answer! So, I figured I would go directly to the source itself! So, who and what are you all about?

From what I've experienced of you, you're this predetermined expectation of how boys and men are "supposed" to be. Growing up, I was constantly told I didn't act like a "boy." That was kind of confusing because I did what other boys did: I played with cars, had a train set, and even played in the mud like other boys!

Well, sure—I played with Barbie. And ... OK, maybe I got caught playing with my mother's heels once or twice. But how was I supposed to know that other boys didn't do the same thing? If the other boys got to play with GI Joe, why couldn't I play with Barbie? So confusing. Then, in high school, I was expected to go hunting, fishing, or play sports because that's what "masculine" guys did. But please—explain to me how those things "prove" masculinity.

If you ask me, it just showed they had the ability and skills to do them. I didn't have the skills or inclination to do *any* of those things. Of which, by the way, regarding sports—can I just say wrestling is *pretty damn gay*! Rolling around on the floor in a tight uniform, grabbing a guy between his legs, and trying to flip him on his back? Yeah, *right*—how does that prove one is "masculine"? Flipping another guy on his back is typically what the top does to the bottom. Plus, those onesies don't leave much to the imagination. They are serious butt-huggers they are, and you can quickly tell if someone is cut or uncut in those things. Seriously, someone may want to rethink the whole "wrestling is masculine" thing!

So, what *does* it mean to be masculine? Am I supposed to be well-built with bulging muscles and an ass you could crack walnuts on? Am I supposed to be intelligent, handsome, polished, and a successful breadwinner? Or am I supposed not to have any feminine traits at all? (Of course, this raises the question of what being "feminine" means.)

For the record, when I think of a masculine man, I think of a built lumberjack in tight jeans with a defined, muscular chest covered with hair. His sweat, dripping in the afternoon sun, glistens as he finishes cutting and stacking wood. (Now that I think about it, I'm not sure if that's my idea of masculinity … or just a fantasy.)

Anyway, I'd greatly appreciate any explanation of what being you means. I don't intend to change who I am, but it would be nice to know who you are.

Thank you,

Not Like Other Men

Dear Homophobe,

I want to take this opportunity to address the malicious words you recently expressed about who I choose to love. I realize you have good old American "freedom of speech," so you can say whatever you like. But please permit me to remind you that I also have the same freedom—despite what you may think. And since you opened the door and expressed your views, I will now walk right on through said door and share my thoughts about you!

In your somewhat well-crafted but hate-filled rhetoric, you mentioned that people who love another person of the same sex are "an abomination to God," and we are repulsive, sickening, and offensive. Subtle.

You've even gone as far as to say we'll "burn in Hell" for our "lifestyle." What exactly do you mean by "lifestyle"? I ask as we live our lives pretty much the same way you do. We are born, go to school to achieve an education for a better way of life, date, marry, create lifelong friendships, divorce, and pursue hobbies that interest us and make us happy. The only difference I can see between us is that you insist on telling us how to live and how disgusting you find us. I find this very perplexing as we don't do this to you or yours.

So, based on your actions, wouldn't you be the one with the different "lifestyle"? Also, when you speak of your God's likes and dislikes, you sound like you are close friends. Have you spoken directly with God, one-on-one? Have the two of you sat down over coffee, and in the course of that conversation, did (s)he (as we don't know if God is a man or a woman) share his or her views and feelings with you on the subject of homosexuals—or any subject for that matter?

And if you have spoken with God, did (s)he ask you to be his/her spokesperson? I ask as you seem to have appointed yourself God's representative. If you are, please provide the paperwork, text, burning bush, or inscribed stone tablet that "appoints" you to such a position. On the other hand, suppose you don't possess any of the previously mentioned items. In that case, I suggest you keep your thoughts to yourself, and your lying mouth shut.

It is none of your business who I, or *anyone* as far as that goes, love, have sex with, or what I or anyone does with their life. I'm not concerned with who you do, so why are you so worried about who I do?

Or perhaps you're repulsed by how many erotic thoughts leap into your mind when you think of my ... lifestyle ... and you are just too afraid to try it yourself. Yes, maybe that's what scares you.

Sincerely,

Mind Your Business

p.s. Please remember that your words of hate have real consequences for those on the receiving end. Words from people like you can result in our death at the hands of others who think it's okay, even valid, to take our lives. Or worse, reflect on those who kill themselves because of self-righteous people like you!

Either way, it's murder by any other name.

Dear God,

We've never officially met. At least, I don't think we have.

I mean, I have had a few near-death experiences, but I don't remember meeting you. Which is a good thing because if we had met, well, we know what that would mean . . . While I'm sure you're nice, if it's all the same to you, I'd rather wait a while before we meet.

Anyway, I know you're busy, so I'll get right to it and ask the question that has plagued humanity for thousands of years: do you exist? Hopefully, that question wasn't too blunt, but I figure an individual in your position would appreciate my direct candor. I hope you don't mind me writing directly to you. I assumed if I wrote to one of your lackeys, I'd probably receive a standard *run-of-the-mill* response: "God exists. Read the Bible. And go to church, you heathen!" Well, that's what I imagine they'd say.

For full disclosure, I have attended church and read the entire Bible—twice. I'll be honest: neither the church nor the bible clarifies my question. In fact, if you don't mind a bit of friendly criticism, the book was of no help at all. It doesn't read well, is inconsistent, and contains numerous variations of the same story, which causes several linear issues with the book's, well, plot.

Then there are the characters: there are too many characters, and we don't get to know their whole stories. Many are superfluous, and most of them, frankly, just don't move the story along! The only character with a backstory is Moses, while Adam and Eve lack any preamble.

Then, and I get that this hits pretty close to home, there is your constant demand to be worshipped. And the ever-present threat of destruction if people don't. Pardon me for stating the obvious, but isn't all that palaver a bit...narcissistic?

I thought *you* were supposed to be a *loving* God! Extinguishing folks doesn't exactly put you in the best of light. I mean, let's have a look. There are numerous instances where you come across as, well, pretty harsh: the great flood, the destruction of Sodom, the whole being lost in the desert, the killing of each first male-born child—and let's not forget the whole circumcision thing. I mean, really, talk about harsh! (I will say I do prefer a nice cut penis over a non-cut one, so I'm a bit split on this one.)

And if you don't mind, I have one more question: how do you feel about gay people? I mean, *all of humanity* is supposed to be your creation, and I assume "all" includes gay people. I ask, as there's a lot of hatred towards us down here on your blue marble. So, if we could get a wee bit of clarity on how you feel about the subject, it would be appreciated.

I know there are lots of questions! But you're one of humanity's great mysteries, so you naturally lend yourself to them.

With kind regards,

Curiosity

P.S. You might find this interesting: Andrew Lloyd Webber turned the story of Joseph and his fabulous coat into a nifty little musical.

You should be enormously proud of that!

Dear Christians,

Your behavior lately has become...problematic. You seem to be splitting into two factions: those who act with love and kindness toward others and another group who have deemed it their role to tell others how to live. Frankly, this latter group is of the utmost concern to me.

You seem to have strayed more than a bit off track from how the Bible says one should act. Correct me if I'm wrong, but doesn't it say you should love your neighbor and let God do the judging? I ask because you seem to be doing the opposite: you judge everyone and tell them how to live, *especially if they don't meet your expectations.*

Why is this? Do you think your viewpoint is more important than what the Bible says? In case you forgot, your little book has over 613 rules on how everyone (repeat: *everyone*)— including yourself— should live. Let's review a few, shall we?

Do not seek revenge,

Do not bear a grudge against others,

Do not eat pork or shellfish,

Do not shave your beard,

Do not touch the skin of a dead pig,

Do not plant two different kinds of crops side by side,

Do not be superstitious,

Do not get a tattoo,

Do not take the lord's name in vain,

Do not wear cloth woven of both wool *and* linen,

...and the list of laws goes on and on.

Pretty demanding if you ask me.

Oh, and let's not forget the big one: "Do not commit adultery." This commandment is so important that your God wrote it down (along with nine other commandments)—in STONE!

So, quiz time: How many of those 613 rules do *you* follow? I ask because many of you do not appear to follow these rules! You shave your beards, have tattoos, are superstitious about your sports teams, and eat pork rinds like they are going out of style ten minutes from now.

Several of you use the Lord's name in vain—especially during sex!

Oh, and let's not conveniently forget the whole adultery thing, shall we? How many of you have cheated on your wives or husbands? And gotten a divorce—despite having been told that "what the God brings together, let no man put asunder," or something like that?

So, if you don't adhere to many of the rules yourself, why do you insist others should? Again, I ask because there seems to be one rule in particular that you insist others follow: "You shall not lie with a male as with a woman ..." (*Leviticus 18:22*)

So, let me get this straight: Out of the 613 rules, *this is the only one you can remember?*

Again, it's rather convenient. Isn't it? If you cling to this rule, shouldn't you also stick to the others? Or do you choose the guidelines *you* want to follow and demand others to adhere to what you say? If you can do what you want, why can't others do the same?

In closing, as you can see, I have lots of questions. That's why I'm reaching out to you. I would love to understand your thought processes better and why you think one law is the only law that should be followed!

I eagerly await your reply.

Sincerely,

Judge Not, Lest Ye Be Judged!

Hello Darkness,

I'm writing to say I've seen you hanging around again! Frankly, this puzzles me because I don't recall extending an invitation to you for a visit. So why do you keep.showing.up?

I don't mean for that to sound rude. It's just that whenever you visit, you bring a dark cloud that envelopes everything and everyone around you. This is of great concern to me because your damn cloud consumes 99% of the energy and happiness that once existed in my life!

Not only that, but your doom and gloomy attitude, refusal to do anything fun, and constant desire to be the only thing in my life make it difficult for me to function. Not to put too fine a point on the whole situation, *but I have friends I like to hang out with and a job I need to be present for.*

To avoid being put into these situations at any time in the future, please don't come around. I know that may sound abrupt, but I'm just trying to ensure you understand where I'm coming from.

Sincerely,

Not Your Friend

REALITY
SETS IN
YEARS

Dear Life,

Um, well, not sure what to say other than That.Did.Not.Go.As. Planned! What the hell happened? I thought we were supposed to be operating with a plan.

I wrote to you years ago about this, and I'm incredibly disappointed I never heard back from you. Anyway, as I stated in that letter, I have to have everything planned in my life. If it's not, I can't function!

Hence, I wrote you so you would know and we could work out—a plan. Think of it as a road map if you will. You know: "Point A leads to Point B. Then, to Point C." And so on. This way, I, and we both know what will happen. Did you plan anything?

No. You didn't!

Instead, I got a series of random mistakes that kept happening, one right after the fucking other! *What happened to the whole idea of an impressive job, a boyfriend that led to marriage, even if we're not legally able to, and then a lovely house and two cute little dogs?*

That's what I *thought* was going to happen. I don't know; maybe I should have shared that thought with you. OK, OK then—that was a mistake on my side. Point granted.

So how about this: I will go with the theory that the last few years have been— a trial run. We were just getting to know each other, figuring out each other's likes and dislikes—that sort of thing. OK?

Now that we've cleared that up, we can get everything back on track, and you can get busy working on that plan, right?

Thank you,

Frustrated.

But Still Ready.

And Concerned.

Dear San Francisco,

Thank you! You've welcomed me with open arms, and I will forever be grateful for what you have done: you've shown me it's okay to be unique and different from other people. From the moment I arrived and began to explore all that you are, I knew I had made the correct decision to leave the small city I grew up in and start anew with you.

I've spent many weekends walking around your bustling streets, discovering many of your hidden treasures: Hayes Valley, Potrero Hill, The Inner Richmond District, Golden Gate Park with the de Young Museum, and, of course, The Castro.

The latter is where those like me can feel...at home.

Here, I can spend hours sitting in my favorite coffee shop—writing, drinking rich, dark coffee, and enjoying the taste and crumble of my favorite pumpkin cookie while watching couples walk by holding hands and showing their love for one another without the fear of being called names, pushed, shoved, or worse yet, beat up for being gay.

San Francisco, you accept *all* people without the evil side eye we often receive in other cities. Although your tall skyscrapers, endless traffic, and multitudes of people milling around can, I'll admit, be intimidating at times, I find they help to create the eccentric energy that fuels the life of The City—and all who call you home. From your charismatic neighborhoods with their unique personalities… to your bustling downtown…and the quiet serenity of Golden Gate Park, you have much within your borders to offer those seeking refuge and acceptance as an equal.

And—I've also uncovered some of your fabled quirkiness: Muni *never* works, BART is the name of the train system and not some guy who slept around the Bay Area, and glitter floats in the air year-round. Probably the most important thing one can learn about you is that, unlike most cities that have four seasons, you have three: winter, fog, and summer (which doesn't arrive until September and only lasts until the last weekend of the month, also known as Folsom Street Fair.) Confidentially, some people claim you do have a fourth season: Christmas. My jury is still out on that one. (But with another pumpkin cookie and some more coffee, who knows…)

When I arrived with my U-Haul and little furniture collection, I was a scared rabbit, unsure of what I had gotten myself into.

But you soon showed me I had nothing to fear, welcoming me warmly like countless others. I will *always* be grateful for your kindness and hospitality, as you have helped me create a life of openness and freedom that I would not have found anywhere else.

Thank you, San Francisco!

Love and forever yours,

Grateful

P.S. I'd greatly appreciate it if you could shed some light on why your famous fog became known as "Carl"? That's always puzzled me.

Dear Cupid,

Hello. I'm checking in to see how things are going from your perspective, as I know how they're going from mine. And, if I can be brutally truthful with you—I get the feeling you're not putting that much effort into this husband hunt because I'm still single!

Don't get me wrong, you have provided an "interesting" sampling of what's out there:

Bald with no hairy chest,

Hairy chest but no personality,

Bald with a hairy chest but nothing where it counts,

Lives at home with his mother,

Just got out of jail,

Maybe a crack problem,

Personality with no looks, and

Looks, with a six-pack and a hairy chest.

That last one would have been great—if you told him I existed. And trust me, I did everything in my power and imagination to get him to notice me. But nothing I did ever worked. I finally got tired of following him around and just gave up. Yes, I know—some would say I might have been stalking him, but I wasn't. We just happened to be at the same place all the time, which I can assure you was *purely* a coincidence.

Then there was the pastor, who had everything: a pleasant personality, a hairy chest, and he was thoughtful and kind. However, the whole religious thing freaked me out. Yes, I know—I said his profession didn't matter, but it was odd going down on a man of the cloth. It felt like God was always going to be watching us. While I don't mind the occasional three-way, that kind of three-way wasn't precisely the one I was hoping for.

Then, of course, there was that married guy, another three-way I had no interest in. What, in The Actual Hell, was *that* all about? I ended up with some pretty severe baggage from that situation. Hopefully, therapy can help me sort through and pack that shit away. Yes, he was married. And yes, I should have said "No." But I thought...actually, I don't know what I was thinking. That was just one big shit show.

Anyway, he and all the others are now in the past, and this "Trial and Experiment" stage of my love life is over, right? *Right?*

You should now have enough information about the type of guys I like to fine-tune your search. Thank you for your time, and please let me know if you need anything else from me.

Sincerely Yours In Therapy,

Still Looking for Love

PS I look forward to the next round of candidates. Well, hang on. On second thought, hopefully, there won't be *too* many. Because the more men I have to sleep with, the more I feel like a whore. That said, I guess I don't have to sleep with *all* of them, but . . . how am I gonna know if we're compatible?

Dear Ms. Cosmo,

I'm in love with you. I've been in love with you since we met years ago on Long Island. I was having an Iced Tea. You sat alone at the bar, poised like Elizabeth Taylor for all your admirers.

All eyes were on you. Your beautiful crimson-red dress sparkled in the crystal that engulfed you. The sun was setting. A gentle Sea Breeze blew in, bringing with it the sweet smell of the ocean.

I tried to approach you. However, I was unsure of myself and ran away like a frightened Greyhound, leaving you to be worshiped by your many lovers.

I left Manhattan, not knowing if our paths would cross again. They did, on the outskirts of Boston. I stopped at a bar, and there you were. Standing tall and proud, looking like you didn't have a care in the world.

This time, you were in pink, which sparkled in the early Vesper night light, the light that only a sunset on Cape Cod can deliver.

Encouraged by my friends, Cpt. Morgan, J. Daniels, and Johnny Walker, I approached you like a lost Pomeranian—Would you feel the same about me as I did of you?

Then we kissed. Our lips fit perfectly. It was the very Last Word in osculation—your smooth edges, sweet scent, and boldness melted my heart and won me over forever... That kiss felt like I'd been hit with a Stinger and reeled back in a Tailspin.

From that moment forward, I knew you were the Bee's Knees, and I would forever be under your spell. The Army and Navy could not pry me from your allure. Indeed, you are the sweet elixir of life, giver of strength and courage, and healer of many broken hearts.

You've nursed this Broken Heart through breakups with Alexander and Rob Roy, job promotions at the Clover Club in San Francisco, and birthday celebrations that left me hangovers that felt like a Moscow Mule had kicked me.

Your steady and constant Warm Embrace helped me on the Vieux Carre that night as I said goodbye to my dear friend while you kept the pain away. I knew then I'd never leave your Safe Harbour—not for all the Martinis in The Bronx.

You've encouraged me to be myself while others tried to diminish my light and bring me down... You showed me how to live as classily as Marilyn Monrow... With you by my side, shining as bright and radiant as Mary Pickford, I know I can achieve my goals and dreams, as you always say yes while others say no.

In the beginning, we enjoyed many nights together as we gazed out over the smooth Sapphire blue sea as the sun transformed its colors from Tuscan yellow to gold, to red, and finally to deep violet until the sea swallowed the sun. Those nights were the most tranquil evenings we shared until that one fateful evening when you met that sex columnist from New York.

One day, you were mine. Then, seemingly overnight, you became the one to be seen with. You were invited to club openings, brunch dates in Martinez, Hollywood premiers, and Southside parties thrown in your honor.

While I know you did not mean to lose sight of our friendship, you couldn't help but be consumed by your new fame. It's been painful having to share you with the world. However, I realize I must, as you are now enjoyed by so many others who find you as intoxicating as I do.

Please know that my heart will always belong to you, my true love.

Yours forever,

Admirer

Dear Passerby,

You walk by with your long, pointed nose raised to the sky. Your head uplifted in an air of superiority. Why do you do this? Is it so you don't have to see what you have created? Smell the stench of those forgotten? I have long ago given up hope of ever being like you again…owning a house, having a job enveloped in the love of others.

The streets are my home now. At night, while you lay your head on a pillow of softness and wrap your body in warmth, I rest my head on the harshness of the pavement and wrap myself in memories of the past, the laughter of my children, the kiss of my wife.

The memory of their love keeps me warm. These memories are also my prison.

Afraid to let go, afraid to move on without them, I confine myself to walking the long concrete corridors filled with pictures and moving images of my former life.

Fighting off the coldness of these streets, I shuffle along, talking to no one, hoping someone will hear me. Do you hear me? I don't want to continue like this; I want to let them go and live their lives, yet I can't. Every face I pass, every smile I see, and the laughter echoing off the buildings and landing in my ears reminds me of them and that day.

I see them screaming my name, calling for me. The ground shook, burning light, the peeling off of my flesh. They were gone, and so was I. I wander alone now, void of any feelings trapped with the death of my family keeping me company. You don't see this. You don't know what I've been through. How could you when you look away in disgust at what I've become?

When they finally remove what remains of me, they will find this letter tucked inside my infested coat. Maybe then you will realize that those you walk over have had families and once longed to be like you.

Sincerely -- One of the Nameless

Dear Heartbreak,

After some deep, personal reflection—and several weekend nights of Haagen-Dazs chocolate chip cookie dough ice cream, listening to Bette, and crying my head off—it's come to my attention that you and I spend way too much time together!

Yes, I know I'm a fun person to be around as I've got a stunning personality, a profound sense of humor, and a fabulous ass, which are all things people find attractive; however, isn't there someone else you'd rather be with? I'm sure there must be somebody out there who is far more fascinating than me.

You know what they say: variety is the key to life, and you'd get that variety if you started seeing someone else. I wouldn't mind if you did; it would benefit us. Actually, it would be good for me if you started seeing someone else. Your constant attention is driving me crazy. You've turned into a little lap dog that follows its owner around, begging for attention and wanting to cuddle. All of the time! While I like both of these, a dog and cuddling, I need some me time! Without you! Just me! While I know you are an inevitable part of life, much like death, taxes, and any of the other assorted feelings and emotions, you, however, are best handled in small doses.

Plus, my waistline can't handle any more of your visits. So, please find someone else to hang out with. I'd greatly appreciate it.

Sincerely,

Expanding Waistline

Dear Vanity,

You have become the epitome of grace, elegance, and sophistication as you possess the "it" factor everyone longs to have, yet you appear to be the only one with "it." From how you move to how you walk to how you talk and carry yourself, you do so with such an exquisite air of confidence that no one can match or surpass your self-assurance.

When you enter a room, it falls silent, and all conversations cease. The last words spoken hang in the air momentarily before falling to the ground as your admirers turn to gaze upon you, seeking your approval and maybe even your praise!

Yet, you don't acknowledge anyone, as you can't be bothered, and so you move on, leaving us mere mortals to continue seeking your recognition. You seem impossible to please.

When we look in the mirror and see gray hair or yet another wrinkle, we will undertake all necessary actions to remove the unsightly blemishes. We dye our hair, buy creams and lotions, inject toxins into our faces, and even go under a skilled physician's bright lights and sharp instruments to obtain that elusive and often desired physical state of being that you alone possess.

Perfection.

What about you causes people to lose sight of their self-worth? Is it because of the grace, beauty, and confidence you possess? Or is it the admiration that you receive from others that we seek? Are you not afraid that someday, people will tire of your constant need for attention and abandon you? One might think your desire to be admired and emulated is a sign of your insecurity. But what would you be insecure about as you have it all, don't you? Are you hiding something behind that façade? If we knew, would we still want to be like you?

Please forgive me for what I'm sure you may consider an excessive number of questions, especially from someone you probably deem unworthy of your time. I can only imagine how much of a burden it is for you to be so admired, adored, and loved as you are.

But, if I may be so bold as to ask you one last question that I'm sure you will only dismiss?

I beseech you to share some of your gifts with me! Allow me, a lowly person with none of your qualities, to help you carry this burden of confidence, self-composer, attractiveness, and irresistibility. While I know I will never be as you are, I would be grateful if you could share a fraction of what you hold.

I remain your humble servant,

Self-doubt

Dear Fate,

Due to a recent event, I was wondering if you could answer a question: how much do you influence events that happen to people, or do certain things happen and you just get credit for it?

For example, two people meet at a gym, which one of them never goes to, and a romance blossoms. Is this something you arranged? Did you influence their choice to go to the same gym, or was it their destiny to meet? If it was destiny, are you and destiny the same? Or was it a coincidence that they met? The latter raises a new issue about coincidence's role in things.

Or, like destiny, are you and coincidence the same?

Here is another example: two strangers bump into each other on their evening or morning commute. After they apologize, a conversation ensues, a date takes place, and a year later, they say their "I do's." Is this your handy work?

Here is another scenario, the same situation: two strangers meet on a subway, a conversation ensues, and then a date ensues. Sounds good so far, but what if one of them is a serial killer, and by the end of the evening, someone ends up dead? Is this your work, or is it just a bad random coincidence? Was it that person's fate to be killed? If so, that just seems fucked up to have your life fated to end at the hands of a random stranger.

Okay, that was dark; here is another scenario: someone stops at their local corner store on the way home and buys a lottery ticket, something they never do. Later that night, when the winning numbers are drawn, they win the lottery. Was it because of you that they won? Or were they just lucky?

Of course, that raises the question, are you and luck the same?

Okay, here is one more scenario: say a famous producer went to an *off, off, off, off, off, off,* off-Broadway play in Duluth, loved the play, produced it, and the play-write went on to win the Tony Award for Best Author (play). Is this your handy work? Is it someone's "fate" to become famous or to succeed at their job? Do you influence all of these things?

If this is the case, how do you pick who will succeed, who will fail, who will fall in love, and who will get murdered? As you can see, I have several questions about how fate, destiny, and luck work. Are you all separate, or do you go by all these names?

Looking forward to hearing from you,

Concerned

p.s. I was recently raped, and, well, I'm trying to make sense of why it happened. Was this something that was "fated" to happen to me? Is there anyone to blame, or do all bad situations fall under the "Shit Happens" category, thus absolving you of all responsibilities?

Dear Anxiety,

I was wondering if you and I could sit down and converse. I ask this because things are getting ... a bit out of hand lately.

Please do not think you've done anything wrong, as you haven't. There are a few things that I think we can work on. Again, please do not read anything into that statement. It's just that all relationships can occasionally use a little readjustment. Please don't get yourself worked up about my previous statement.

Although saying that will get you worked up anyway, please know that's not my intention. You do not need to worry about anything we need to talk about. I'm probably just making things worse by mentioning that we must speak.

Since writing to you is probably worsening the situation, please let me know your earliest availability to proceed with a face-to-face meeting. Would you like coffee sometime soon?

With love,

Angst

Dear Depression,

Sorry for taking so long to figure out who you are. I did not realize the darkness and emptiness that consumed me, were you! You've done an excellent job of masking your true identity.

I had no idea it was you.

Anyway, it's come to my attention that you have taken up residency and moved in with me! I'm unsure how this could have happened because I don't recall ever asking you to be my roommate. Was I drunk one night and asked you to move in? If so, please know that was a mistake, or I think it was a mistake.

At this point, I'm not sure.

I mean, before you arrived, I was perfectly okay living alone. I had my friends and an active social life. I did things. Since you've taken up residence, all that has changed. You've shown me that being at home all the time has its advantages; I'm able to save a shit load of money by not going out, as there are no dinners, cocktail hours, or coffee dates with friends to go on—just night after night at home with you, alone.

But is this solitude a good thing, though? Don't you want to be social? Meet people? I'm sorry, I shouldn't ask that question because you've made it clear several times that you do not want me to go out. But don't you think I should at least let my friends know what I'm doing instead of just not returning their calls? I know, you're going to say I shouldn't bother them, which you're probably right, as they have their life to live, and I don't really have a life to live.

You're probably right.

I would just be bothering them. Maybe having you live here is a good thing, as I won't worry my friends as much, and they can continue their fun, happy lives. I'll just . . . be here. With you.

If there is anything I can get you, please let me know. Not doing anything is a good feeling.

Thanks,

Your New Roomie

THE QUEST
FOR PEACE
YEARS

Dear Life,

Are you drunk?

I ask because that is the only reason I can think of to explain your recent behavior.

One minute, you're happy and joyfully skipping down the street, singing to the birds as if you don't have a care in the world. The next minute, you're spiraling out of control, screaming, crying, and falling face down in the gutter, only to jump back up and continue your day as if nothing happened.

What is wrong with you? Your out-of-control behavior and mood swings are giving me whiplash!

So, I'm going to ask no; I'm going to plead with you one more time to please pull your shit together and get back on track with how my life is supposed to be operating: ON A PLAN!

I can't function unless there is a plan, and I've repeatedly written to you about this, and yet you seem to be ignoring my letters because this chaos called my life continues. And for the record, yet once again, I must say that this is not functional for me!

If you think about it, having a plan does make sense. It's functional, there are no surprises, you know exactly what's going to happen, and more importantly, especially for me, it eliminates my anxiety!

So, since this is my life, shouldn't it be functional? I get that you have a carefree attitude and like to go with the flow, which is excellent for you.

However, this doesn't work for me. It never has.

So, please, can we get back on track with how things should be: an outstanding job, a husband, two dogs, and a lovely house? I already have dogs because I couldn't wait for you to figure things out.

So, do I have to stage an intervention with you to help you regroup?

Why am I even asking?

You're going to say no and that everything is fine. I can assure you, it's not! OK! Please, I'm begging, Pull Your Shit Together and Figure It Out!

I know that's somewhat blunt, but if you grew up with my mother, you'd see that she wasn't the most gifted linguist and tended to tell it like it is, which, as you can see, she passed down to me.

So, Pull It Together and Get Back to The Plan!

With love,

Concerned

Dear Cupid,

I'm at a loss for words at this point, but I will try it anyway.

For years, I've seen my friends go from one-night stands to dating, relationships, engagements, and eventually, marriages, ending up in a thrupple (i.e., dating a third person with their husband).

And then there's me. Picture this: I am sitting at home on a Friday night ... listening to Adele ... eating cake (which I baked!) ... and watching action movies where everyone dies. Why, you ask?

Because!

I'm!

Still!

SINGLE!

Correct me if I'm wrong, but aren't you supposed to fly around and shoot your little love arrows at people to assist them in their quest for love? Well, Sport, I hate to be the one to tell you, but so far, you are able to hit everyone else with your "arrows" but me! Perhaps you need to get your eyes checked? Just saying'...

I mean. Honestly! I ask because, as far as I can tell, yours truly could be standing in an empty 100-acre field, with nary a soul nor a plant nor a tree near me ... *and you'd still manage to hit someone in a town a hundred miles away!*

If it helps, I'd be more than happy to make an appointment for you with a Licensed Optometrist. Or an Ophthalmologist! Or for Pete's sake an Otolaryngologist! *How about a Voodoo Priestess?!*

(Repeating to myself: "Blood pressure! Blood pressure!")

Hell, I'll even drive you to the appointment!

This way, I can make sure your eyesight is satisfactory.

And for all that's Holy and Divine (besides my ass...) if it's not your eyes—*then what, for the love of God, is it? My breath?*

Surely, I haven't done something to piss you off, have I? I mean ... lately. Sure, I may have written a few plays in which you were depicted as a, well ... *(cough)* ... drunk, useless cherub sans pity who broke into someone's house. But...*but*...I wrote those plays as comedic *odes* to you and your ... *wonderful* ... skills in finding true love for people. I can assure you, in all honesty, that they were probably not meant as a dig for your inability and total, complete, and utter failure to find me a husband! ... *"Blood pressure! Blood pressure!"*

("It's OK. I'm better now...") Perhaps this is all just a silly mix-up, and you lost my address? Yeah, sure, that's got to be it!

I mean, Mom warned me I shouldn't have moved so much, and so maybe she was right! *(Don't tell her I said that - the woman is insufferable as it is.)* For the record, you are to blame for my relocation habit as I kept moving in the hope that a bigger pool of men would help you in your... hunt... as you'd have more men to shoot your arrows at.

Obviously, that theory didn't work either.

Wait! Maybe you forgot the type of guy I like. If so, here it is again: bald, hairy chest, and a dad bod! Let's face it: that's probably all I can get these days. I could probably get someone with a six-pack, but that would cost me a fortune, and I'd rather spend my money on other things, like a trip overseas or better blood pressure medication.

He should be taller than me or the same height. The constant bending over to kiss a shorter guy would irritate my lower back, and at my age, I have enough body ailments. Thank you. Oh, and he needs to be able to laugh at my jokes, as my sense of humor is all I've got these days. There's a rumor going around that I have "some" mental sanity remaining, but damned if I'd swear to that...

Anyway. Where was I? Yes, 'tis sadly true: The body of my twenties and thirties seems to have packed up and left me in its rearview mirror.

So! There you go! Let's start with round four and hope for the best.

Sincerely,

Still Looking for Love (and my rumored sanity...)

...Film at 11.

Dear Crush,

I have no idea what I was thinking when I agreed to organize our high school reunion. I thought it would be fun because I hadn't seen or talked to anyone in years. If it hadn't been for Facebook, I probably wouldn't have, but seeing everyone pop up on my feed piqued my interest, and I thought, what the hell, I might as well do it.

Well, to be honest, I wanted to see how everyone had aged over the years (it turns out some of them had aged poorly), and I was hoping you would show up.

The night went pretty much as I thought it would: a bunch of "Hi, how are you doing!" and "How are the kids?" and "You got a divorce, sorry to hear that." Throughout the evening, I did the customary small talk—and was only insulted a couple of times because some people still hadn't changed and thought calling me names was fun.

I made a few casual inquiries about you, as I didn't want to raise anyone's curiosity. But no one knew where you were, if you were single, or if you would even show up. Hours later, and much to my delight, you walked through the door! And yes, once again, my heart skipped a beat.

You wore your standard tight-fitting jeans, tight shirt, and cowboy hat, a new accouterment. It adds to your appeal, or at least I think it does. You are as good-looking as you were in high school, your blue eyes still shining brightly, and your golden blond hair had just a hint of grey at the temples.

I held off on approaching you for as long as possible, but I gave into temptation and had to talk to you. Your voice still had that strong, confident tone I remembered from the night we studied together.

After exchanging a few pleasantries, and before I could inquire further about how you had been over the years, your adorable wife made a beeline toward us to steal you away. I wish we had more time to catch up that night, but it was evident that someone had other plans for you. Did she know?

Or was she just being her typical self: Queen of the Bitches, just like she was in high school? Whatever her reason, I still got to spend a few minutes alone with you, and memories of what could have been flooded my mind.

What if? I will forever wonder if something could have happened that night.

Sincerely,

Fond Memories

PS - Could something happen now?

Dear Venus,

First, I'd like to say I'm a major fan of yours; you are just divine.

I saw Botticelli's painting, "The Birth of Venus," in Florence. It was breathtaking! As are all the other paintings and statues created as a homage to you that I've mooned over the years. I am sure—it is a fact that no other woman can hold a candle to your beauty. Not Elizabeth Taylor, Angelina Jolie, or even Madonna herself.

No, not *that* Madonna—the pop star Madonna. Of course, these days, she is a bit of a train wreck and has pretty much destroyed her career, face, and fan base.

But forgive me, please? I digress.

I just want to say you are *heavenly*, which explains why you are the Goddess of Love, as only someone as stunning and serene as you can be. And it is because of your magnificence that I am writing to you. I hope you can help me with a specific part of my life that seems to be going nowhere: my love life.

I've previously written to your son. However, to date, I have not received any, shall we say, front-runners in my quest for a husband from him. But I beg you, please don't take that as a criticism of his undoubted abilities! I am sure he's simply too busy helping others in their quest for love to help me. Or perhaps my letters have gotten lost in the mail. Or maybe the neighbor's dog at them. Or possibly they were stolen by that kid who lives on the corner. The one with the nasty streak in him...

If any of those are true, well then, that explains a lot.

As I was saying.

I was wondering if perhaps *you* might be able to assist me instead. I've been searching for this elusive husband for some years now, and as you know, in the gay world, the older you get, the less appealing you are to others. And I hate to say this, but at my age, I have more yesterdays behind me than tomorrows in front of me. Or, not to put too fine a point on it, I am getting up there in years.

A twink, with no body fat, a six-pack (...*I don't mean beer*), and a nice happy tail, will always win out over someone who's balding and has a bad back. (i.e., me.)

Over the years, I've seen numerous friends win the trifecta of date-engaged-married as I sat, third row left on the aisle, with a wilting corsage and no love in sight, coupled with world-class calluses on my hands. (And between me and you and the bedpost, if you knew some of these people, you'd be as shocked as I am that they found someone—anyone! *Half of these people are far more needy than I am!*)

I mean, I'm a cute, honest, straightforward guy with a keen sense of adventure, sensuality, and humor seeking someone of the same caliber. With a hairy chest.

Yeah, while I may have a...*few*... issues, but I can honestly say most of my "stuff" is gracefully packed away in matching Louis Vuitton luggage and stored neatly in the garage.

In closing, My Beautiful One, I do hope you can assist with my search for a husband. I would forever be grateful to you if you could.

Your Humble Servant with High Blood Pressure Still,

Looking for Love

P.S.

A twink is a gay slang term for a young or young-looking man who is gay or bisexual. Twinks are usually in their late teens to twenties and may have the following traits: a slim to average physique, a youthful appearance, little or no body hair, flamboyancy, and general physical attractiveness.

Dear Death,

I realize that a visit from you is inevitable in one's life. However, I was unprepared for what your visit would entail, especially when they were back-to-back. *Shit!*

Your visits have left me devastated, and the loss teeters on unbearable. How could you do this? You have taken the two I have loved the most in this world. Actually, you didn't take them. You forced me to watch them be given to you.

Do you realize the sorrow and anguish you have caused me over the last six months? It was bad enough that I had to make that decision once. But turning around and putting me in the same situation just several weeks later is unforgivable! That decision will haunt me for the rest of my life. I will never forgive you and will despise you for the rest of my life.

The past six months have been the worst of my life, starting with that fatal week when he woke me in the middle of the night in severe pain because he could not urinate. His sad little face looking at me, begging for help. I couldn't do anything! I rushed him to the clinic and asked them to save my little boy. Hours passed before the doctors returned to tell me his tiny bladder had stones causing his pain. The surgeon removed them, but that would not be the end of it. The surgery resulted in an infection throughout his body, one that he could not shake. By the end of the week, his weight had dropped, he was not eating or drinking, and you forced me to make the decision. And the doctors—looking at me with blank, manufactured sympathy. What else could I do? I was brutalized! But I could not endure seeing him in such agony. My heart broke into a million little pieces that night.

But you sick, unfeeling bastard. You were not done with me.

In less than three months, my other baby got sick. He was unable to walk comfortably and was in pain at the slightest touch. Over the next several weeks, I watched as his health deteriorated until that last morning—when he awoke with breathing problems. I knew then that you were about to pay me another visit, and by the end of that evening, I was holding him in my arms as he slowly drifted off to sleep and across to you.

Why so soon?

Why so soon?

WHY SO SOON!?

Could you have given him... and us... *just a little longer?*

Being forced into resolving to end the lives of my kids were two of the most horrific, indescribably tortuous, soul-sucking decisions I've ever had to make. And while their pain is over, mine continues. Daily.

I come home to an empty house. No cute little faces or wagging tails to greet me. Instead, the stillness of the grave and the scuff of my shoes across the floors of a heartbroken house. I sit here, alone, empty, and in despair. Pain and sadness thrust their razor talons and bottomless beaks into me over and over, picking, gorging, feasting, tearing at the last few remnants of a once joyous heart. Every glance at a blanket, a leash, or a bowl drives tears from my eyes until I have no more to give.

I beg of you, please don't revisit me for quite some time. You son-of-a-bitch.

Sincerely,

Shattered

Dear Sex Life,

Yo! Hey, are you OK?

I am somewhat concerned as I have not heard from or seen you in some time. Is everything copacetic? Have I done something to ... offend you? If I have, please let me know so we can discuss it! I'd like to get back to where we used to be. I mean, we used to be pretty close. But lately . . . what happened?

Remember the fun times we used to have? Like when we went to the grocery store for some eggs and milk—and instead, came home with Magnum P.I.! It wasn't him, but it's always been a great fantasy of mine all these years later to think that it was...

Then there were those twins. Whoa! Sadly, not at the same time. But still—they were kind of fun. And they did end the debate on whether twins are/were "identical." Turned out—they were not!

Then there was the newscaster. We met him before he went to work for CNN. We were curious, unsure what happened to him, and never saw him on air.

Oh, and remember the two guys from New York? I met one in New York for business and the other while I lived in San Francisco. It was a surprise to find out they knew each other. Even more of a surprise when we found out they.hated.each.other! What are the odds of meeting two guys on opposite sides of the country who knew (and hated) each other? Good times…

That story has always been great to entertain people at parties. Yes, I talk about you at dinner parties. Don't worry, they were gay dinner parties, so the conversations always centered around someone's sex life. Remember my 28th birthday party? That was a wild night!

We've had so many fun encounters over the years, but I hardly hear from you these days. What happened? Why did the fun stop? Was it because I got sidetracked with other things? Did you just give up on me?

I have so many questions about your departure. I hope you will take the time to reply to this letter, as I would love to hear from you.

Looking forward to your reply and returning to where we left off.

Miss you!

Yours Always,

Sexless in The City

p.s. Would a little blue pill help? My treat!

Mi Amore,

You have captivated the minds and hearts of man for thousands of years. Poets have written sonnets adorned with melodious praises and euphoric excitement on the way you have touched their hearts.

Plays have been written exploring the anguish and delight you can bring to one's life. Thousands of songs have been sung in your praise and speaking of your virtues. Others tell of the sorrow and agony you can inflict.

You have toppled rulers, kings have given up their thrones in your name, and others have built monuments to honor you for the happiness and joy you have brought to their lives. You are the most revered and yet the most feared one in the world.

Why is this?

Is it because of the complex emotions one encounters because or despite you?

People have described you as a feeling of delight, pleasure, warmth, and complete bliss. Yet you are also described as a sensation of discomfort, apprehension, and deep anguish. How can you be all of these at once? And if you are all of these, how is it that you garner so much interest and admiration...while being so devastating at the same time? The pain and the hollowness felt when you depart are said to be nigh unbearable. People describe it as the ground suddenly disappearing and a vast emptiness consumes them. The discomfort you bring seems to last longer and be more severe than the pleasure you brought in the first place.

How can you abandon someone knowing what your absence will do to them?

This brings me to an important question, so please excuse my bluntness, but what *are* you actually? Are you a feeling, an emotion, an action? Do you even exist materially? If you do exist, where do you exist in us? Some say you exist in our hearts, but how can this be? The heart is a muscle used to pump blood through our bodies, and yet when someone experiences the loss of you, they say they have a broken heart because you no longer envelop them in your warm embrace. That does sound excruciating.

The strong reactions you elicit in people cause me to sit in bewilderment and awe of those who have experienced you. The sheer mention of your name causes me to lose my breath and become numbed with fear—not because of the pleasurable feelings you can bring, but because of the power of hurt, emptiness, and loneliness you can also field.

Honestly, I don't think I've ever experienced you. Are you worth the pain you can cause?

Sincerely,

L'Amore e un mistero

Dear Anxiety,

For the love of Baby Jesus, please take a chill pill and relax. I'm sorry for being direct, but sometimes, the best way to deal with an issue *is* to be direct.

For the sake of our survival, you need to take a step back, sit down, and take a few deep breaths. Your constant paranoia, apprehension, and habit of reading crap into every little thing the way you do has gotten out of control.

Initially, it was a minor annoyance as I thought it was your way of getting me to think through my decision-making process. These days, it has gotten so bad that you question everything and everyone around you, which has put us in a constant state of nervousness. I can't do anything without believing people are thinking something horrible about me, or I second guess a decision so many times and think through every possible outcome that I end up unable to make any kind of a decision.

It's exhausting!

Please know that what I'm about to say is meant with love—but this behavior needs to stop. Not everything is as layered as you think, except people. People are complex, *multi*-layered, and sometimes enigmatic.

Moreover, here is their core issue: we will never know what others are thinking, so why bother trying? Everyone has problems. Most folks are probably overthinking things just as you are!

So, with that thought in mind, let's stop trying to figure others out and, as an alternative, work on ourselves to get our thoughts back on track to being reasonably happy and living our lives the way we want without fear of what others think. Yes, some people will always judge us and tell us we are doing something wrong. However, that speaks more to them than to us.

If we are being our *true selves*—without consciously hurting others—we're doing the best we can. And that must be as good (*rewarding* and *pleasing*) as possible.

So, I beg you, let's work on changing our situation so we can experience how bright and carefree life can be without worrying about everything! I'm here for you. We can do this—and we can do it together. I promise I will hold your hand and be with you every step of the way.

We can conquer this!

With love,

Angst be Gone

Dear Voices,

First, I'd like to take this opportunity to ask if you'd please quiet down. You've been pretty active as of late, and it's rather tiresome and annoying because you keep interrupting every part of my life with your constant chatter.

Please S-T-O-P!

I realize you may not know this but reviewing something that happened twenty-odd years ago at 3:00 AM is not a productive use of our time. We should be sleeping at 3:00 AM.

Yes, for God's sake, failing that math test in college *could* have been avoided if we had studied. Granted! And yes, maybe I should have said something different during that interview. And yes, maybe, possibly, perhaps I should not have sent that text to the guy. But ship-sailed and all that, I did, and there is nothing we can do about it now. I already messed things up!

Next!

So, I know this is an odd request coming from me, especially since I have a tough time moving on, but can you please stop bringing up these things —and that colorful laundry list of other things—from my past? I, we, need to rest. Why do you keep bringing these things up?

Do you have something against sleeping?

Do you have something against me?

Do you like to torment me?

Or are you just friggin' bored!?

If the answer is yes to the last three questions, please don't bother me! Instead, why don't you try thinking about what it would be like to have a good night's sleep? Better yet, enjoy the sweet fragrance of petunias carried into the house on a gentle summer breeze. Or simply enjoy a moment of nothingness. You might find you enjoy it.

Thank you,

The Search of Quiet

Dear L.S. Esteem,

You first came into my life many years ago when I was a young, impressionable kid, which was just what you were looking for: someone you could mold and manipulate. While other kids' parents were protecting them from the likes of you, my parents, most unfortunately, were not able to provide this security for me as they were busy fighting each other in their divorce. In their absence, you could maneuver your way into my life, where you reveled in your ability to control how I viewed myself.

Proof? Not a day went by when I didn't hear you whisper that I was worthless, that I wasn't good enough for anyone, that I'd never be a success, that I wasn't loveable. I tried to believe otherwise, but your whispers turned to shouts to reinforce what you had always told me. That I was ... *n o t h i n g!*

For years, I tried not to listen to or believe what you said, but over time, you broke me down to the point where I couldn't help but believe there was truth to what you were saying.

I was in such a state of despair that I couldn't leave my apartment. I thought the outside world did not want me. When I could venture out, I didn't look or speak to others. How could I? I heard your voice telling, shouting, *and shrieking at me that I was unworthy and* not attractive and that others didn't want to spend their time talking to a worthless waste of oxygen like me!

One evening, your deceit reached a crescendo when ... I contemplated giving up on everything. As I resolved to do so, I heard a small, earnest voice telling me not to give up. Telling me I was worthy, I was valuable. For the rest of that night and many nights afterward, that's all that glorious voice whispered to me, "Don't Give Up!"

And I did not.

About that time, in those dark mental hallways, you reunited me with your cousin Confidence, who in turn introduced me to Hope. They told me I was worthy, valuable, loved, and that things would get *better*!

Confidence repeated and repeated those words until I finally listened and started to believe in myself. With her continued help, I can now walk with my head held high and a stronger belief in myself. Hope has allowed me to see a light at the end of this journey. Confidence helped me see the value I hold as a person—something you always wanted to extinguish.

So, heads-up, Chump.

With this newfound inner strength, I can now tell you that you no longer hold *any* control or influence over me. No longer will I live in such a disheartened state because of you. I *am* a worthy person! I *am* important! I *am* loveable! And I damn sure love *myself!*

And that is something you will never break. Ever.

Adios!

I am Worthy. And. Valuable

Dear Depression,

I always considered myself a strong person who would never allow someone to control me. Yet that is *precisely* what I allowed you to do.

You told me who I could see and what I could do, and you wanted— no, you demanded—to be the only one in my life. And I stupidly and unfortunately allowed you to become just that.

I gave up my family, friends, and everything I enjoyed appeasing you. For years, we lived together surrounded by your dark cloud of emptiness and loneliness, which suited you and what you wanted, but it left me empty and alone. Every time I tried to break free from your control, you constantly told me I couldn't survive without you. Foolishly, I believed you because I didn't know any better, nor did I think I could. You and everything you wanted consumed my whole being for years until that one fateful night . . .

A night that has had a profound effect on me and has brought about the end of you and our relationship. One I profoundly regret *ever* getting involved in. For the last several months now, I've been reading books, reading articles, reflecting, and practicing mental health exercises to regain what I gave up because of you: myself!

Minute by minute.

Hour after hour.

Day after day.

Month after month.

I have been repairing myself. Telling, informing, and believing...

I AM A GOOD PERSON!

Telling myself that I *deserve* to live.

That I *deserve* a life surrounded by light, happiness, and beauty.

And now, because of the work I have put into myself, I can tell you... *no...*, I *demand* that you leave! NOW!

Our relationship is fucking over! And contrary to what you said, I *can* live without you! And that is *precisely* what I will do—in style.

The darkness you once surrounded me with and your habit of consuming every ounce of happiness I have reached their end. You are no longer welcome here. I've packed your belongings, carried them out the front door, and set them on the street for the garbage man to retrieve, which is precisely where you belong—in the trash.

Your time in my life is over! While you may think I will cave in and allow you back, I can assure you this is, nor will it ever again be the case. I have cut out all habits that might allow you to flourish. No longer will I listen to your lies or your deceitful ways of trying to control me. You are toast, Jack. You are done.

Vacate the premises. Now!

And...don't let my door hit you in the ass, either.

Sincerely,

I. Am. Enough

MY TRUE
SELF YEARS

Dear Life,

You know, this whole journey would have been easier if you had told me at the beginning to have patience. If you had, do you know how much "extra" drama we could have avoided? I wouldn't have had so many freakouts, I might not have written so many letters, and maybe, just maybe, I would have dealt with things better than what I did . . .

Okay, who am I kidding? I'm unsure what the word "patience" really means! Being a Type "A" personality makes it challenging to have faith in anything I can't control. And you know ... I do not do well if I can't control everything.

I'm sure this stems from some horrible event that happened in my childhood that should have been unpacked in therapy. But it wasn't. For the record, I made several attempts at treatment. I just couldn't find a therapist I 'fit' with. Hence my continued need to control and map out *everything* in my life. I now realize it was/is pointless because you showed me repeatedly that I would *never* be able to do that. I was just too stubborn to admit it.

So, as much as it kills me to say this ... you win.

I hereby give up on all my efforts to live my life "planned out." I finally accept that you have been guiding this crazy adventure we call "my life" this whole time. *Are you happy now?*

I also admit I should have given up on that idea long ago, especially since we ended up in the same spot anyway. I've got a great job I like, I'm making enough money to buy a house, I've got a great circle of friends, I can finally travel abroad, and I'm finally starting my writing again.

So, I was wrong, and you were right.

Ugh! Honestly, you don't know how much it pains me to say that.

With that in mind, I will now (*somewhat reluctantly*) say ... thank you for sticking with me despite my numerous breakdowns and the multitude of letters I wrote you (especially the whole drunk comment one.) Sorry about that.

While I'm sure you might plan more twists and turns for me in the future, I think I can finally deal with what you throw at me. With that said, please don't throw too much!

I kind of like the way things are now.

Thank you,

Content

P.S.—If I can make one tiny request of you, how about we utilize at least some kind of... outline instead of a plan? This way, we'll at least know where we're going.

I just thought I'd throw that out there. Please get back to me when you can. I appreciate that.

Dear Closet,

It's been a while since we last spoke, and much has happened since I heeded your advice to live genuinely. And live I have—what a whirlwind it's been!

I came out. I became a top drag queen in my hometown. I moved a few times (okay, several times). I harvested a great circle of friends. I played softball ... traveled to Europe ... went to Australia ... had a job, lost a job, and changed jobs. I went to school and got a degree. I had sex. I had some great sex. I had some not-so-great sex. And I even had some "What the hell was *that?*" sex. I tried dating. No dice. I lived with someone. No dice.

But now...

I have a great job. I'm still single (damn you, Cupid). I'm in Palm Springs, living a life that once seemed like a distant dream, accompanied by my four adorable Chihuahuas, enjoying this serene poolside with a glass of exquisite Italian wine in hand.

I also write to share another significant milestone: I'm finally pleased to embrace my feminine side. Yes, I know saying I'm "finally embracing" this side of myself sounds odd, especially considering it's my predominant nature. But I've always been afraid to do so because of the way people treated me growing up. Being called faggot, queer, and being physically assaulted for acting like a girl left me feeling like everything about myself was wrong.

I wanted to be liked and to be loved.

Contrary to what people may think, I didn't allow myself to follow my natural interest in anything feminine. Yes, I did drag, but that was a performance that allowed me to pursue my interest in feminine things. But when the wig came off, so did the character, and it never blended into the rest of my life. The two stayed separate.

But all that changed when Billy Porter wore a dress to the Oscars. Until then, it never occurred to me that following my natural interest in things deemed feminine was an option or a possibility for me. But when I saw Billy Porter being his true self, I began questioning ...Why *wasn't* I being my true self and true *to* myself?

The answer is staggeringly simple: fear. Fear of what others would think of me. I was still holding on to the thought that I couldn't be "myself" because others (definition vague....) wouldn't "like" me.

Bull.

I chose to liberate myself from the shackles of fear, to step out in my pumps, and to embody my true self with *pride*. The external changes—manicured nails, sculpted eyebrows, the luxury of a genuine Louis Vuitton purse, and, yes, the fashionably painful pumps—are mere evidence of my inward revolution: I Am No Longer Afraid to Be Me.

I've realized that judgment will follow regardless of my path, so why not tread the one that leads to self-fulfillment and joy? Your wisdom—that I should live on my terms, guided by my heart—has become my mantra.

Today, I stand liberated, living as my true self, unapologetically and without fear.

With heartfelt gratitude and newfound courage,

My True Self.

Dear Love Life,

It was with a sense of somber reflection that I recently laid a rose upon your symbolic final resting place.

I had meant to visit earlier. However, I was simply unable to bring myself to do so. I could not face the fact that ... you had finally passed away. I guess the occasional date, a few brief conversations with guys, the rare smile from a stranger on the street, and a few clicks on Grindr from "military" men in Kabul were not enough to sustain you.

I would say your untimely demise caught me off guard. But was it untimely?

Or was it inevitable that you would finally succumb to the wounds you received from this new "dating app" world? Swiping right became the thing to do because the next swipe always held the potential to reveal ...him! But did it? Really? Or did it just turn into an endless game of hope and self-deception-meets-mental-masturbation? Because no one took the time actually to see a person. Everything revolved around what one "looks" like, not about who or what one "is."

I did my best to support you in the glare of this slot machine dating game. I went to the gym to create a body that others would find appealing. I gained weight. I lost weight. I gained muscle. I lost muscle. I tried to be butch. I stopped doing drag.....

Hell's Bells—I even tried to (*Lord Jesus, save me!*) play sports, and we both know how that went! I still have a slight limp from that bad slide into second base, and my voice never has recovered from being hit in the throat with a "softball." And that was just from practice! All that supports our efforts to make someone stay on our Grindr photo and *not* swipe right.

Ultimately, my efforts were ... fruitless, and I apologize for that. Hell, I'm sorry for everything. I don't know what else I could have done.

Though a whimsical part of me imagines your return, perhaps as some kind of romantic revival, I'm well aware that the love life resurrected would be akin to a zombie—better left as a chapter closed. *:sigh:*

So, with a heavy heart, I bid you *adios*, mourning the loss of what we once had and the memories of those rare but cherished moments of genuine intimacy. I will always cherish that long-ago kiss and that enthusiastic night of lovemaking we had with our "Friend With Benefits" all those years ago.

Sincerely,

Love Don't Live Here Anymore

PS Hey? Maybe you're not dead—but you are in a trance like Sleeping Beauty! And maybe you'll return with a true love kiss? One can hope...

Dear Cupid,

Well, I guess it's time I face the inevitable fact that this whole love thing is not in the cards for me. You've tried. I've tried. And yet—I've always been a bridesmaid and never the bride.

Well, I was always the usher and never the ... well, you know.

Since love seems to have gone out the window headfirst (along with my youth and attractiveness), I have finally come to grips with the fact that I'm going to be an old queen wandering around Palm Springs in a convertible, wearing fabulous caftans with big sun bonnet hats to shield myself from the sun, with "Chihuahuas Ala' Rhinestone Collars" in tow.

Which, if I think about it, doesn't sound so bad. I've always looked good in a caftan, and that will probably be the most comfortable outfit to wear in that heat.

Anyway, thank you for your time and effort,

Still Looking?

Dear Masculinity,

I have spent years trying to figure out who you are, and I am no closer to solving this mystery than I was when I first started. You are an enigma—a puzzle that cannot easily be solved. I know as much about you as I know about the moon's backside.

Why is that? (Well, not the moon part...) Why is your identity so vague?

All I know is that for years, both the straight and gay communities have told me that I don't act like you, that I act like a girl, and that I'm too effeminate. But neither constituency can provide me with a definition of who you are. The straights can't define you because, for them, you are based on some ancient notion of what a man should be. To the gays, you are some overhyped-up sexual fantasy drawing created by Tom of Finland. And no one can measure up to an entire community's sexual fantasy. I mean, damn—based on those two concepts, I was/am *never* going to fit into anyone's idea of what being "masculine" is. The one element both communities agree on is that "men" are not supposed to have "feminine" characteristics. And if they do, then they better watch it, or they will be deemed ... undesirable.

That leads to this question: Isn't the whole preoccupation and belief that boys and men are supposed to act one way and girls and women are supposed to act another a bit ... archaic?

Why do boys have to be masculine? *Why* do girls have to be feminine? And *why*, on God's Green Earth, can't either sex just "be"? Sans labels? If boys want to play with Barbie—so be it. If girls want to play football—so be it.

Let's just say it: the idea of "masculinity" is out-of-date. It's based on an out-of-date assumption that "men" are the more vigorous sex. These days, one's strength is no longer strictly judged to be a "physical" attribute. These days, it is more (correctly) about a person's inner drive and determination, regardless of the chromosome lottery.

Women have become quite "strong," in my definition because they have had to fight their way out of being dominated by "masculine" men and more than a few ill-informed women. Then there are those men, like me, who get their nails done, walk with a swish in their step, shape their eyebrows, and act in a way that society says is "feminine."

Our folks have always been deemed "not masculine" because of the way we act/appear. Yet many of us live on our terms—and do not welcome others' ideas of how we should "act." It takes a strong person to live their life that way. Especially considering the condemnation one can receive for doing so.

So, which is truly the strong, masculine person? The individuals who think Penis=Superior/Stronger? Or those who have had to fight to live on their terms despite the adversity they receive from the world for doing so? And which gender are they?

Thoughts?

Feminine and Proud

Dearest Ms. Confidence,

Please accept my apologies for this letter's tardiness. I should have written to you some time ago, but it's only recently that I've found myself free of the troubles that have prevented me from doing so.

As you know, I was most unfortunately in two somewhat toxic relationships with two of your cousins: Low self-esteem and Depression. Both relationships had me wrapped in a cloud of darkness that nearly destroyed me. If it hadn't been for you, they would have succeeded. You came back into my life on a night when I was ready to give up on myself and everyone around me.

However, you refused to give up on me. In your glamorous, forceful way, you came roaring back into my life and told me not to give up—to continue going on. You sat me down and reminded me of who I am. Through your sheer perseverance and with the help of your other cousin, Hope, you combined to help me once again discover something I had forgotten: my unique voice as a human being.

You reminded me of this for weeks until I started to listen, and then you recapped everything I'd accomplished in my life: coming out to friends and family, having the strength to pluck and tuck to become an outstanding female impersonator, wearing heels and showing other women in the shoe department how to work them, returning to school, getting my degree, and taking to the stage again as a writer, producer, and actor.

You repeatedly reminded me of these and several other achievements I had forgotten. You helped me regain my strength, the voice of my humanity, and a belief in myself that I had given up on. How can I ever repay this debt? Your words helped me to step back into the light and break free from those painful relationships.

While I occasionally hear the odd whisper or two from your down-side cousins, their words are like specks of dust that linger momentarily in the air and are carried away on the wind—as they should be.

Thank you once again for giving me back to me.

Forever grateful,

Me

Dear Depression,

Good afternoon. I felt it was time to update you on my progress since our parting. Your departure has, frankly, been a revelation for me, bringing forth a chapter of my life rendered in brighter hues than I had dared to imagine possible.

Since our separation, the renovation of my life and overall health has been profound. I've turned my attention inward positively, dedicating myself to constructing the existence I've always aspired to. My living space is now a testament to this revitalization: the kitchen sparkles, dishes are neatly stowed away, and my pantry and fridge boast selections that are as nourishing as they are delightful. Clothes once strewn about in despondent disorder have been laundered, folded, and neatly organized, although I confess, the ironing awaits necessity's call.

I've invited vibrancy back into my home by adding colorful plants, throwing open the curtains to bathe my world in natural light, and eradicating the dust and cobwebs accumulated from the deserts of my previous neglect. These changes have cleared the physical space I occupy and significantly alleviated my allergies, marking a literal—and metaphorical—breath of fresh air. *Danke!*

My existence has been liberated from your shadow, allowing me to embrace life with a newfound ease. Your pervasive doom and gloom, which once stamped my environment, has been dispelled, replaced by an ambiance you would find utterly repellent. That delights me.

Reconnecting with friends has reinstated joy and a sense of belonging that I had sorely missed, and our rekindled relationships stand as witness to my companions' understanding and support— fortified by a mutual commitment to prevent any recurrence of my isolation.

In conclusion, removing you from my life ranks as one of my most significant achievements. I have arisen from darkness into a world awash with light, possibility, and hope. The joy I now experience is profound—and genuine.

In closing, not only can I survive without you, but I can, indeed, thrive. This letter is not just an update; it is a declaration of my independence and a testament to the resilience of the human spirit.

Sincerely,

A Devoted Fan of Myself

Also, I've noticed another of your cousins, the Doldrums, out and about lately. I hope you are not using him to get back into my life. I know you think I'll take you back, but rest assured, I will not!

Dear Grief, my unexpected companion,

As your visits have increased in frequency, I feel compelled to pen this letter to acknowledge our growing acquaintance—a relationship born of circumstance rather than choice and one that fills me with a profound sense of trepidation.

Please do not misinterpret my words. My dread stems not from disdain for you but from the dreadful prelude to your arrival, heralded by your cousin, Death. Death's visits always signify the loss of someone (or something) dear, leaving in his wake a sea of sorrow, anger, and despair.

In the initial throes of our encounters, I could scarcely differentiate between you and Death, so overwhelming were the symptoms of your presence. This confusion delivered a fear of your arrival, which persisted until a recent revelation: you and Death are not the same but exist as distinct entities.

While Death brings the storm of grief, you follow with a lantern of solace, guiding us through the emotional turbulence that ensues. You are the navigator helping us chart a course through the murky waters of memory and loss, leading us gently toward the dawn of healing. In your presence, we find the courage to sift through our shared past, discovering peace amid the storm of our tears.

Without your guidance, the weight of our grief might well engulf us. For this, I extend my heartfelt gratitude. Though your visits are born of loss, they are not confined to the death of loved ones. You also stand by us as we navigate the end of friendships, the dissolution of romantic ties, and the shattering of dreams—reminding us that endings, in all their forms, are a necessary, essential, and natural part of life.

You teach us to bid goodbye to valued hopes and to embrace the journey ahead, bereft of what we once held dear. In moments of parting and loss, you are the embrace that fortifies us, enabling us to process our emotions and continue forward.

With this understanding, I recognize the value of your presence—a presence to be appreciated, not feared. I offer sincere apologies for the misconception I once harbored. Thank you for your unseen work, helping us untangle the complex web of our emotions.

With gratitude and newfound respect,

A Student of Grief

PS Though I accept our future meetings, I venture to make a request: could you space your visits further apart? Their frequency of late seems, if I may say so, a touch excessive. I remain ...

Dear Happiness,

Recently, you sparked quite a debate between my friends and me. We had just settled into our villa outside of Florence, lounging poolside with wine in hand—a scene as idyllic as one could imagine. The lush green hills of the Italian countryside rolled into the distance, punctuated by the spires of an ancient cathedral. A gentle breeze carried the sweet scent of Bougainvillea while the evening sky painted itself in shades of lavender, lilac, and mauve against the backdrop of a fading golden sun. At that moment, surrounded by friends in what seemed like a painting come to life, I declared, "This is probably one of the happiest moments of my life." And thus began the lively debate about your nature.

Opinions varied widely; some saw you as a fleeting emotion, while others argued you were more of a tangible sensation. The distinction between a feeling and an emotion was debated—though, to me, they seem intertwined. Some mused if you were a transient state of being, here one moment and gone the next, while the more cynical among us questioned your existence altogether. Such diversity in understanding, yet each perspective shares the common thread of seeking you out. Some questions then if you please?

How long do you linger if you are indeed a state of being? Are you a brief interlude or a lasting presence? As a feeling, do you resemble the joy of watching a clumsy puppy, the awe of beholding a newborn, or the thrill of a new purchase? If an emotion, are you the smile that unwittingly graces our lips at the sight of a loved one or the tears that spill over in moments of unbridled joy?

There are so many questions, yet no definitive answers. For me, you are the magic of an Italian sunset, the camaraderie of a meal with friends, the celebratory sound of a wine cork popping, and, most significantly, the sense of triumph over personal battles.

Thank you for the moments when I have genuinely felt you,

In a good place

Dear Hope,

This is just a brief note to assure you that you haven't faded from my view. You remain constant in my heart—a beacon guiding me ever forward.

Your presence is a steady reminder of the core lesson of your teachings: the light at the end of every tunnel, the silver lining of every cloud.

Thank you for being my untiring companion.

With gratitude,

Hopeful

Dear Self,

Just a little reminder as we navigate our journey together:

I've got your back.

I cherish you deeply.

And the most beautiful chapters of our story together are yet to be written.

With all my love,

Me

ABOUT THE AUTHOR

Inspired by Carrie Bradshaw, Rodney Taylor returned to school to obtain their degree in writing and graduated from San Francisco State University with said degree in Creative Writing.

Not sure what (s)he wanted to do with it; after all, who knows what to do with their degree? (S)he meandered about their writing career aimlessly for the first year until a friend suggested they join a writing group focused primarily on plays. Their writing career soon took off.

(S)he soon found themselves writing, producing, and acting in plays, which was new to them. They went on to write the short plays *Eros, Poolside, Good-Bye Cupid, Fairy Godmother, Baby Christina, Motherly Advice,* and *P.S. I Love You.* Their playwriting eventually led them to co-found Left Coast Theatre Co., an LGBTQ theater in San Francisco with Joe Frank.

After a bad career move left them pondering life, they took a few years off writing to focus on themselves and bring them back to a "happy" place.

These days, they are focused on their mental health and resuming their writing career. No longer concentrating on plays, they are branching out and exploring their interest in comedic short stories.

At the same time, they traverse the country with their "one" Chihuahua until they find their forever home, hoping that Cupid will still pay them a visit. Hopefully after a visit to the optometrist...